DISNEY

✦ PRINCESS

Happily
Ever After
Stories

Disney
PRESS

New York

TABLE OF CONTENTS

CINDERELLA
My Perfect Wedding 5

THE LITTLE MERMAID
Ariel's Underwater Adventure 29

BEAUTY AND THE BEAST
Getting to Know You 51

ALADDIN
The Mysterious Voyage 75

ALICE IN WONDERLAND
Alice's Tea Party 85

SNOW WHITE AND THE SEVEN DWARFS
Two Hearts as One 111

CINDERELLA II: DREAMS COME TRUE
Aim to Please 135

TABLE OF CONTENTS

THE LITTLE MERMAID
Ariel and the Sea-Horse Race 161

BEAUTY AND THE BEAST
The Teapot's Tale 171

ALADDIN
One True Love 195

SLEEPING BEAUTY
A Moment to Remember 219

ATLANTIS: THE LOST EMPIRE
Kida and the Crystal 243

CINDERELLA II: DREAMS COME TRUE
An Uncommon Romance 271

THE LITTLE MERMAID
Dreams Under the Sea 297

Designed by Alfred Giuliani

Collection copyright © 2004 Disney Enterprises, Inc.

"Alice's Tea Party" adapted by Tennant Redbank from the original book *Walt Disney's Alice's Tea Party* by Lyn Calder and illustrated by Jesse Clay copyright © 1992 Disney Enterprises, Inc.

Disney's Beauty and the Beast: "The Teapot's Tale" adapted by Justine Korman and illustrated by Peter Emslie and Darren Hunt copyright © 1993 Disney Enterprises, Inc.

Disney's The Little Mermaid: "Ariel's Underwater Adventure" adapted by Michael Teitelbaum and illustrated by Ron Dias copyright © 1989 Disney Enterprises, Inc.

Disney's Atlantis: The Lost Empire: "Kida and the Crystal" adapted by Amy J. Tyler from the original book *Kida and the Crystal* by K. A. Alistir and illustrated by the Disney Storybook Artists at Global Art Development copyright © 2001 Disney Enterprises, Inc.

Disney's Aladdin: "The Mysterious Voyage" by Liza Baker and illustrated by Robbin Cuddy copyright © 2001 Disney Enterprises, Inc.

Disney's The Little Mermaid: "Ariel and the Sea-Horse Race" by Sarah Heller and illustrated by the Disney Storybook Artists copyright © 2002 Disney Enterprises, Inc.

"Aim to Please" and "An Uncommon Romance" adapted by Amy J. Tyler from the Walt Disney movie *Cinderella II: Dreams Come True* copyright © 2002 Disney Enterprises, Inc.

Artwork for the following stories was created by the Disney Storybook Artists:

"One True Love" written by Annie Auerbach. Based on the characters from the movie *Disney's Aladdin* copyright © 1992 Disney Enterprises, Inc.

"Dreams Under the Sea" written by K. Emily Hutta. Based on the characters from the movie *Disney's The Little Mermaid* copyright © 1989 Disney Enterprises, Inc.

"My Perfect Wedding" written by Lisa Ann Marsoli. Based on the characters from the movie *Walt Disney's Cinderella* copyright © 1950 Disney Enterprises, Inc.

"Getting to Know You" written by Lisa Ann Marsoli. Based on the characters from the movie *Disney's Beauty and the Beast* copyright © 1991 Disney Enterprises, Inc.

"Two Hearts as One" written by Catherine McCafferty. Based on the characters from the movie *Walt Disney's Snow White and the Seven Dwarfs* copyright © 1937 Disney Enterprises, Inc.

"A Moment to Remember" written by Catherine McCafferty. Based on the characters from the movie *Walt Disney's Sleeping Beauty* copyright © 1959 Disney Enterprises, Inc.

All rights reserved. No part of this book may be reproduced or transmitted in any form or by any means, electronic or mechanical, including photocopying, recording, or by any information storage and retrieval system, without written permission from the publisher. For information address Disney Press, 114 Fifth Avenue, New York, New York 10011-5690.

Printed in the United States of America

First Edition

10 9 8 7 6 5 4 3 2 1

This book is set in 20-point Cochin.

Library of Congress Catalog Card Number: 2003096530

ISBN: 0-7868-3487-0

For more Disney Press fun, visit www.disneybooks.com

Walt Disney's Cinderella

My Perfect Wedding

Cinderella's dreams were coming true at last! With the help of her mouse friends, she had managed to race down the stairs just in time to let the Grand Duke place the glass slipper on her foot.

Now she
and the Prince
were going to be
married, and their
brand-new life
together filled
with happiness
would soon begin.
But first there
was a wedding
to plan. . . .

Cinderella didn't have the faintest idea where to begin.

Prudence, who ran the castle household for the King, was happy to take charge. She sat with Cinderella and read off a long list of things that needed to be done for the wedding.

"Excuse me, Prudence," Cinderella said as soon as Prudence had paused for a moment, "but couldn't the Prince and I just have a simple wedding?"

Prudence frowned. "Cinderella, now that you are going to be a princess, you must start thinking big!"

Later on, the Royal Dressmaker arrived with several wedding gowns. The first gown was covered with bows and sashes. "The guests will mistake me for a present!"

cried Cinderella.

"You look just like *a princess*!" Prudence said.

"Do you think you could design something plainer?" Cinderella asked.

"No!" Prudence

exclaimed. "*Plain* and *princess* do not go together!"

The next day, Prudence and Cinderella visited the castle's royal florist shop. The Royal Florist greeted them with . . . a bush! At least Cinderella thought it looked like one.

"This is lovely," she said, "but do you have something a bit smaller?"

"It's perfect," Prudence said. "You just have to know how to carry it." She held the flowers out in front of her—and was stung by a bee!

That afternoon, the mice found Cinderella all by herself in the garden.

"Where's bossy lady?" asked Gus.

"Poor Prudence," replied Cinderella. "She got quite a nasty sting from that bee. The Royal Physician says she must stay in bed for the rest of the day."

"But what about the wedding plans?" Jaq asked.

"I'll just have to take care

of them myself!" Cinderella declared. "Now, what should I do first?"

"Who'sa comin', Cinderelly?" wondered Jaq.

"The guest list! Good idea, Jaq. Let's see. Well, of course, all of you are invited," Cinderella replied. "And my Fairy Godmother . . . Actually, I wish she were here right now."

And almost as fast as Cinderella wished it, her Fairy Godmother appeared! After giving Cinderella a big

hug, she said, "I just *love* weddings— the beautiful gown, the towering cake, the romantic music. And I'm sure everything you've picked out is just lovely!"

Cinderella admitted she hadn't actually picked out anything yet.

"And when is the wedding, dear?" asked the Fairy Godmother.

Gus counted on his fingers. "Tomorrow!" he announced.

"Oh, my goodness, child!" cried the Fairy Godmother. "Then we'd better get started!"

"Lots ta do!" Jaq added. He and Gus unfurled Prudence's list for the Fairy Godmother to see.

"We'll plan an absolutely magical wedding for you, dear!" the Fairy Godmother gushed. "Now, let's begin with the dress." With a wave of the Fairy Godmother's wand, Cinderella was instantly adorned in an elegant

white gown. But her Fairy Godmother had forgotten the veil.

"It's beautiful," Cinderella said, "but don't you think it needs . . ."

But the Fairy Godmother wasn't listening. She had already moved on to the next item. "Invitations!" she declared. In the blink of an eye, hundreds of lovely cards sat in stacks around the room.

"Now we shall prepare the feast and make the cake!" the Fairy Godmother announced. "I want everything to be perfect!"

Cinderella changed back into her blue dress and followed the Fairy Godmother to the royal kitchen. Meanwhile, the mice stayed behind, picking up

where the Fairy Godmother had left off. Mary, Suzy, and Perla lifted some scissors and cut a small piece of fabric from the long train of Cinderella's wedding gown. Then they threaded needles, pulled out a box of tiny pearls, and went to work on a veil.

"Invite-tations!" Jaq announced. Instantly, the mice lined up, and each received an armload of cards to deliver throughout the kingdom. They didn't get very far before their plans were spoiled by Pom-Pom, the castle cat!

"Whew! Close-a call!" cried Jaq as he and Gus raced away from Pom-Pom and caught up with Cinderella in the castle kitchen.

"And now for the best part!" the Fairy Godmother announced. Cinderella watched as her Fairy Godmother squeezed her eyes shut in concentration. Then, with one grand sweep of her

wand, the Fairy Godmother created the biggest, fanciest cake Cinderella had ever seen.

"What do you think?" the Fairy Godmother asked.

Cinderella, trying to hide her disappointment, said evenly, "Um . . . Prudence will love it. And speaking of Prudence, I really should go see how she's feeling."

"Poor child," said the Fairy Godmother after Cinderella had left. "I think all these wedding plans are too much for her."

Jaq and Gus tugged at the Fairy Godmother's sleeve.

"Cinderelly like smaller things," Jaq told her.

Gus pointed proudly to himself. "Like mice!"

All at once, the Fairy Godmother understood.

Later, in Cinderella's chamber, the Fairy Godmother

took Cinderella's
hands. "I'm afraid I
may have gotten a
bit carried away,
my dear," the Fairy
Godmother con-
fessed. "Now tell me,
child, what would
the wedding of *your*
dreams be like?"

After listening to Cinderella, the Fairy Godmother began to perform her magic. With a wave of her wand, the hundreds of tiny pearls the mice were stitching onto Cinderella's veil were scwn into place. Then she sent the invitations out the window to their destinations.

"Now let's cut that cake down to size," the Fairy Godmother said, with a twinkle in her eye. But before the two

departed for the kitchen, Cinderella stopped and looked tenderly at the kindhearted mice. "Thank you, my little friends," she said gratefully.

The next day, Cinderella looked lovely in her simple white gown, veil, and gloves. In her hands she carried a small bouquet of garden flowers that the mice had gathered for her.

But just as the King was about to escort her down the aisle, Cinderella looked down and gave a little cry of surprise.

The Fairy
Godmother followed
the bride's gaze. "Good
heavens, child!" she
exclaimed. "You can't
get married in your
bare feet!" She waved
her wand, and two
glass slippers peeked
out from beneath
Cinderella's gown.

After the ceremony, the Prince and Cinderella shared a joyous celebration with their guests. It was the most wonderful wedding anyone in the kingdom could ever remember. Even Prudence was pleased.

"How ever did you manage all of this?" the Prince asked his new princess.

Cinderella smiled and said, "With friends by your side, anything is possible!"

ARIEL'S UNDERWATER ADVENTURE

One afternoon, Ariel was hunting for human treasures in a graveyard of old sunken ships with her best friend, Flounder.

"Come on, Flounder!" shouted Ariel as she swam

into one of the ships. "Let's look in here."

"Are you sure it's safe?" asked Flounder.

"Sure," answered Ariel. "Follow me."

Inside, Ariel found a chest full of treasures.

"Oh, Flounder!" Ariel gasped. "Have you ever seen anything this wonderful in your entire life?"

Inside the chest, Ariel found a fork and a pipe. "This is great!" the Little Mermaid cried. She put the objects into a pouch. "I don't have any of these in my collection yet!"

Just then, Flounder heard a noise. "W-what was that?" he cried.

"I didn't hear anything," said Ariel, who was too busy looking for more treasures to notice any strange sounds.

Trembling with fear, Flounder peeked outside the doorway of the ship. There, with a huge mouth full of sharp teeth, was a shark.

"Shark!" screamed Flounder as he raced back
inside.

Ariel grabbed her
bag of treasures.
She and Flounder
swam quickly to
the upper deck.
The shark followed,
snapping its jaws.
Ariel and Flounder

squeezed through one of the ship's portholes.

Ariel and Flounder thought they were safe, but the

fact that the porthole was too small for the ferocious

shark to fit through

didn't stop it for a

minute. It crashed

right through the

side of the ship

and continued

after them!

The mermaid

and her little

companion were swimming as fast as they could. But they could barely stay ahead of the shark's terrible jaws.

Then the shark lunged at Ariel and Flounder. It missed them, but its strong jaw snapped the ship's mast as if it were a matchstick.

Ariel and Flounder swam as fast as they could toward a huge old anchor that was wedged in the ocean floor. The shark was right behind them, snapping all the way.

"I hope this works," Ariel said with a gasp.

"M-me, too!" cried Flounder.

When they reached the anchor, the two friends slipped through the ring at the top. The shark tried to follow, but it was too big to fit through. It was stuck!

"Let's get out of here," said Ariel. "We can head up to the surface to show Scuttle my new treasures."

On the surface, Ariel and Flounder visited with their

friend Scuttle the

seagull. Ariel pulled

one of her new

treasures out of

her pouch.

"Do you know

what this is?"

Ariel asked

Scuttle, handing

him the fork.

"Why, certainly," replied Scuttle. "After all, I'm the world's greatest expert on humans. This is a . . . a dinglehopper. Humans use it to straighten their hair, like this." Scuttle ran the old fork through Ariel's hair.

"What's this, Scuttle?" asked Ariel, handing him the pipe.

"This is most definitely a . . . a snarfblatt!" he answered. "It's used to make music." Scuttle blew into the pipe, but nothing came out except water. "Hmm. Nothing worse than a defective snarfblatt!" he cried.

Ariel didn't care if the snarfblatt worked. She was just excited to have more human treasures to add to her collection.

She and Flounder said good-bye to Scuttle and headed to Ariel's secret underwater cave, where she hid all her human treasures.

Suddenly, the cave got very dark. Ariel looked

up and noticed something on the surface of the

water, blocking out the moonlight.

"I'm going to see what that is, Flounder," said Ariel as she began swimming away. Flounder followed Ariel.

On the surface, they saw a very big ship.

"How beautiful it is!" she exclaimed. "We've got to get a closer look."

Ariel and Flounder swam over to it. Scuttle, who
had also seen the ship, flew over for a better look, too.
Ariel and Scuttle reached up and peered over the side

of the ship while Flounder
looked on from the water
below.

Ariel saw a young man.
He watched as his shipmates
were singing and dancing.

"I've never seen a human this close before," said
Ariel to Scuttle.

"He's very handsome, isn't he?" she added, looking at the young man the sailors called Prince Eric.

"He looks kind of hairy to me," said Scuttle, eyeing Prince Eric's sheepdog, Max.

But Ariel didn't hear Scuttle. All she could think about was the handsome young man she had just seen. Ariel was falling in love.

Suddenly, without warning, a big storm came up. Rain poured down, lightning flashed, and the wind tossed the ship like a toy boat. Ariel watched Prince Eric as he and his crew tried to keep the ship afloat.

As the ship tossed and turned in the water, a bolt of lightning struck the mast. The burning mast collapsed onto a keg of gunpowder. The explosion threw Prince Eric overboard into the raging waves.

"The prince!" shouted Ariel.

Prince Eric sank under the water. Ariel knew that if she didn't act at once, her handsome prince would drown.

Ariel dived into the sea. She grabbed Prince Eric and brought him back up to the surface. Holding him tightly, she swam to shore and dragged him onto the sandy beach.

While the prince lay sleeping, Ariel stroked his hair

and sang him a beautiful love song. How Ariel wished she could be with Prince Eric in the human world!

Before the prince began to stir, Ariel heard his ship-mates coming. She knew she had to leave before she was seen by the humans.

Blowing the prince a kiss, Ariel turned and dived back into the ocean.

Ariel and Flounder returned to her secret cave. The Little Mermaid looked around at all her treasures.

"Oh, Flounder," said Ariel. "Prince Eric is so handsome. I can hardly wait until I see him again."

Flounder just smiled.

Ariel combed her hair with her dinglehopper and wished for the day when she would be with her human prince forever.

Disney's

Beauty AND THE BEAST

GETTING TO KNOW YOU

Belle placed a blanket over the sleeping Beast, as Mrs. Potts, the teapot; Cogsworth, the mantel clock; and Lumiere, the candelabrum, looked on.

Maybe the Beast has a heart, after all, thought Belle. That day, he had rescued her from a pack of wolves. Even though the Beast was angry with Belle for leaving the castle, he had risked his life to save hers.

"Maybe I could try harder to be his friend," she told herself.

Everyone was hopeful that Belle and the

Beast would fall in love so the spell—cast by an enchantress that had turned the castle's inhabitants into household objects and the Prince into the Beast—would be broken. Then they'd be human again!

That night as Belle sat by the fire reading, Mrs. Potts gathered Lumiere, Cogsworth, and her son, Chip, and went to find the Beast. He was in the West Wing,

gloomily staring at the rose the enchantress had left behind.

"Master, it's such a chilly night," she said. "Why not have a nice, hot drink in front of the fireplace?

I'm sure Belle would love some company."

"I'm sure she doesn't want *my* company," the Beast grumbled.

"Now, now, come along," insisted Mrs. Potts. "You never know. Surely, it's better than being shut up here all by yourself."

Reluctantly, the Beast followed.

He stomped into the sitting room and settled into a chair.

"Good evening," Belle said.

The Beast did his best to smile as he picked up his cup of cocoa.

Belle went back to reading until she was startled by a loud *SLURP*. She looked over at the Beast, who had a large chocolate mustache on his shaggy face.

After a nudge from Mrs. Potts, the Beast stopped

slurping and slumped in his chair.

Mrs. Potts tried to change the subject. "Why don't

you read to us, dear?"

she suggested to Belle.

"All right," replied

Belle. She turned

to a new story in

the collection of

fairy tales she was

reading.

"Once upon a time there was an old woodcutter—"
Belle began.

"That sounds so boring!" interrupted the Beast.

"Perhaps if you were more *patient*—" Belle said.

But Mrs. Potts gently interrupted.

"Is there another story you could tell

us?" she asked.

Belle flipped through

the pages until she found a

tale filled with fire-breathing

dragons and brave knights.

The Beast sat on the edge of his seat, listening to every word. It pleased Belle to see that the Beast enjoyed a good story as much as she did. She also noticed that when he drank his cocoa, he was careful not to slurp.

The next day, Lumiere and Cogsworth decided to play matchmaker, too.

"What a beautiful day for a walk!" Cogsworth exclaimed after breakfast.

Belle and the Beast looked out the window. It was gray, cold, and windy.

Belle looked bewildered. "Do you really think so?" she asked.

"What's the point of taking a walk?" challenged the Beast. "Walking is useful only when you have some-where to go!"

But before Belle and the Beast knew it, they were bundled up and herded outdoors.

"There's nothing more romantic than a walk in the snow," said Lumiere dreamily as he watched the two disappear into the woods.

The Beast and Belle walked along in uncomfortable silence.

Then they came to a mud puddle, wide and deep. Belle stood there, deciding how to make it across without becoming completely drenched. A gentleman would carry me over—or at the very least spread his cloak across it, Belle thought, suppressing a giggle at the very idea. Clearly, the Beast would do neither.

"Oh, well, here goes," Belle said to herself, as she waded across the puddle. Her skirt, coat, and boots were soon covered in mud.

The wind picked up, and all at once it started to
snow. "It looks like a bad storm is coming," the Beast
warned, looking up at the darkening sky. "We'd better
get back while we can still see where
we're going."

Quite unexpectedly, the Beast took
Belle's hand. "Follow me!" he commanded,
leading her through the blizzard.

Belle was relieved when, a few minutes
later, they arrived safely at the castle.

Lumiere and Cogsworth were watching

out the window as the two approached, Belle's hand

firmly grasping the Beast's paw.

"How romantic!" exclaimed Lumiere.

A few minutes later, Mrs. Potts and the Wardrobe

were helping Belle out of her muddy clothes. "It looks as if you and the master are getting to know each other better," said Mrs. Potts. Belle hesitated. "I suppose," she answered. "There is so much about him that's gruff and rude . . . yet he's full of surprises."

In another part of the castle, Cogsworth and Lumiere were helping the Beast dry off. "Did you have a nice time?" Cogsworth asked.

"Well," the Beast began, "Belle can be rather boring and proper. But then she walked through the mud without complaining. And she didn't act scared at all when we got caught in the storm. She's . . . kind of surprising."

That afternoon, Mrs. Potts prepared a lovely lunch and served it in the greenhouse. She thought the

beautiful room was the perfect romantic setting for the pair's budding friendship.

"Remember, master," Lumiere said to the Beast beforehand, "young ladies appreciate politeness."

"Try to be understanding,

Belle," begged Mrs. Potts before Belle went into the greenhouse. "The master's manners aren't always what they should be—but he's trying!"

The dining companions entered the greenhouse and sat stiffly at the table. Belle forced a smile, and the Beast managed an unconvincing grin. Both were tired of trying to be on their best behavior.

When Mrs. Potts had gone, the Beast began to devour a chicken leg.

And after Belle made a big display of picking up her napkin and placing it in her lap, the Beast hurriedly grabbed his own napkin and did the same.

"Isn't this lunch delicious?" asked Belle.

"*Mmpffgrl*," answered the Beast, his mouth stuffed with food.

Just then, the Beast noticed his napkin on the floor. As he ducked down to retrieve it, he knocked the table over, sending the lunch crashing to the floor. A roll even flew off his plate and landed in Belle's lap!

Even the Beast knew throwing food was not polite. He was about to apologize when he saw a playful smile spread across Belle's face. To his surprise, she pitched the roll right back at him!

BEAUTY AND THE BEAST

When Mrs. Potts, Lumiere, and Cogsworth came to
check on the pair, they couldn't believe their eyes. Food
was everywhere, and, even more peculiar,
Belle and the Beast were laughing!

"What's going on?" Cogsworth
whispered. He pushed the door open a bit
more so they could all get a better look.

"Maybe they're in love," Lumiere said
hopefully. "When people fall in love, they
always seem to behave a bit strangely."

Mrs. Potts smiled knowingly. "I think

they discovered what we forgot: the real way to make friends is to relax and be yourself!"

That night, Belle and the Beast shared a perfectly wonderful dinner. Afterward, Belle patiently taught the Beast how to dance. He listened carefully to everything she told him, and soon the two were gliding across the dance floor . . . in step with each other at last.

Disney's Aladdin

THE MYSTERIOUS VOYAGE

Aladdin and Jasmine had just gotten married. And now the newlyweds were preparing to take a romantic trip far, far away.

"Jasmine is going to be so surprised when she sees what I've planned!" Aladdin said to his pet monkey, Abu. "She has lived most of her life within the palace walls. Now we're going to see the world . . . together!"

Soon Aladdin and Abu went to pick up Jasmine. "Madame, the Magic Carpet awaits you," said Aladdin.

"Won't you tell me where we're going?" Jasmine asked as she took his hand. "I'm dying of curiosity."

"You are going to see things you've never ever seen before—a new, exciting world," Aladdin replied.

"Let's get going," said Jasmine. "I can't wait!"

Jasmine, Aladdin, and Abu took off, soaring high above the palace, leaving Agrabah behind.

"Look how small everything looks!" Jasmine cried.

"It's like a dream."

After a little while, the Magic Carpet began its descent. "Are we there?" asked Jasmine.

"Almost," said Aladdin. "I want this to be a surprise."
He reached forward and
covered her eyes.

"No peeking!"
Aladdin told her.

Suddenly, the
Magic Carpet
landed on top of a high
cliff. Jasmine heard a loud noise that sounded like
crashing water.

"Can I look yet?" she asked excitedly.

"Open, sesame!" cried Aladdin. "This, Jasmine, is the ocean!"

Jasmine couldn't believe her eyes. She had never ever seen anything so beautiful! Dolphins leaped in and out of the brilliant turquoise water. In the distance, huge waves crashed onto a white sandy beach.

"This *is* another world!" said Jasmine, happily. "I've read about the ocean, but I can't believe I'm actually seeing it!"

They had a wonderful time swimming and enjoying the sun. Finally, it was time for their next destination.

"Will you tell me where we're going?" Jasmine asked.

"That would ruin the surprise!" exclaimed Aladdin.

"But I promise it will give you the chills."

Aladdin told Jasmine to cover her eyes. Suddenly, Jasmine felt the air grow colder. A warm coat was placed around her shoulders.

"You can open your eyes now!" Aladdin said excitedly.

This time, everywhere that Jasmine looked, she saw white!

"This is snow!" cried Aladdin. "It falls from the sky when it's cold."

"It's amazing!" cried Jasmine. "It looks like a soft white cloud!"

They spent the rest of the day playing in the snow. They even used the Magic Carpet as a sled to slide down a nearby hill over and over again.

Soon the sun began to set, and the air grew even colder. They climbed onto the Magic Carpet and headed back to Agrabah.

"You've shown me places so different from Agrabah," Jasmine said happily. "There are so many brand-new worlds for us to share."

As they made their way back to the palace, Jasmine smiled. She knew that this was just the beginning of their wonderful life together.

Walt Disney's

ALICE in WONDERLAND

ALICE'S TEA PARTY

Alice was sitting in a tree with her cat, Dinah, listening to her sister read a book out loud. Actually, Alice wasn't *really* listening. She was busy making a daisy chain and playing with Dinah.

Suddenly, a white rabbit hurried by, looking at his pocket watch and yelling, "I'm late! I'm late! No time to say hello. Good-bye! I'm late!"

"He must be going somewhere important," Alice said as the tardy bunny disappeared into a large rabbit hole.

Alice was very curious, so she followed him into the hole. She had crawled only a little way when she found herself falling down, down, down.

She landed in a strange place with magic mushrooms, talking flowers, and some very unusual creatures. And that place was Wonderland.

"I must find the White Rabbit," Alice said. She began walking and came upon a gate in the woods. Behind the gate was a large house with a thatched roof.

Alice stepped through the gate and saw a long table. The table was set with all kinds of teapots, cups, and saucers. The teapots were whistling a merry tune—and they were dancing, too!

Alice's eyes opened wide.

Then she heard voices

singing a very strange little song about unbirthdays.

Suddenly, Alice noticed a gentleman wearing a tall

green hat. He was the Mad Hatter. And next to him,

wearing a red jacket, was the March Hare.

Alice was very thirsty, so she decided to sit down.

The Mad Hatter and the March Hare continued to sing. When the song ended, Alice clapped.

"No, no, no!" cried the Mad Hatter, just noticing Alice. "You can't sit there!"

"It's rude to sit down without being invited," said the March Hare.

"It's very, very, very rude," piped a little Dormouse from inside a teapot.

"I was enjoying the singing so much," Alice explained.

"You enjoyed *our* singing?" asked the March Hare.

"What a delightful child!" cried the Mad Hatter.

"Please join us for a cup of tea." He pointed to a cup

that had somehow become stuck to his elbow.

Then the March Hare poured tea into another cup.

"I'm sorry I interrupted your birthday party," said

Alice, reaching for

the cup.

The March Hare

pulled back the cup of tea

before Alice could take it.

"This is an *un*birthday party," said the Mad Hatter.

Alice looked puzzled.

"It's simple," the Mad Hatter told her. "There are three hundred and sixty-five days in a year. If your birthday is one day, that leaves three hundred and sixty-four unbirthdays!"

"That means today is *my* unbirthday, too!" cried Alice.

"What a small world," said the Mad Hatter.

The Mad Hatter and the March Hare both began to sing, and the teapots started whistling and dancing again.

When they had finished, the Mad Hatter pulled a cake out from under his hat. "For you!" he said to Alice. "Now make a wish and blow out your candle."

Alice wished that she would find the White Rabbit, then blew out the candle. The cake sailed off the table

like a rocket and exploded into fireworks. *Kaboom!*

"Now, is there any way we can help you?" asked the Mad Hatter.

"Why, yes," said Alice. "I'm looking for the White Rab—"

"Clean cup! Move down!" cried the Mad Hatter

before Alice could finish what she was saying.

"But my cup *is* clean," said Alice. "I haven't even

taken a sip."

"It doesn't

matter! Move

down!" the

Mad Hatter

cried out.

Then he and

the March Hare each took Alice by the hand and led

her around the table.

Once they were settled in their new seats, the March Hare poured Alice another cup of tea. But the Mad Hatter put too much sugar in it. When Alice took a sip, she got a sugar mustache.

"So, how can we help you?" asked the Mad Hatter.

"It all started while I was with Dinah, my cat. . . ." Alice began.

"Cat!" cried the Dormouse, popping up from the teapot. He raced around the table until the Mad Hatter caught him and put him back in the teapot.

"Get the jam!" yelled the March Hare. "Put it on his nose!"

As Alice spread jam on the mouse's nose, the March Hare handed her another cup of tea.

But as soon as Alice had lifted the cup, the Mad Hatter called, "Clean cup! Move down!"

The Mad Hatter and the March Hare each took one of

Alice's hands and once again moved her around the table.

"Continue your story," said the March Hare.

Alice was tired of moving down and not getting any

tea. But she still wanted to find the White Rabbit, so she

continued her story.

"I was sitting with my . . ." Alice didn't want to say

 "cat" for fear that she would
upset the Dormouse again,
so she whispered the word
to the Mad Hatter.

"Tea? Did you say tea?" said the Mad Hatter.

"Is half a cup all right?" asked the March Hare. He used a knife to cut a cup right down the middle. The Mad Hatter poured some tea into one half, and somehow it stayed inside.

But Alice still didn't get to drink anything because the March Hare took the cup and drank it himself.

"Would you care for some tea?" asked the March Hare.

"Yes," said Alice, "but—"

"Well, if you don't care for tea," the Mad Hatter said, "you could at least make polite conversation."

"I *have* been trying," said Alice. "I'm trying to ask about the White—"

"Wait! I have an idea!" interrupted the March Hare. "Let's change the subject!"

Alice couldn't believe her ears as the Mad Hatter asked a riddle about a raven and a writing desk.

"I haven't the time for this," said Alice, rising.

"Time? Time? Who's got the time?" asked the March Hare.

Suddenly, Alice heard a familiar voice.

"No time! I'm late! I'm late!" said the White Rabbit as he hurried by.

"Wait! I want to talk to you!" cried Alice.

She started to run after him, but then remembered her manners.

"Thank you for the tea!"

Alice called over her shoulder to the Mad Hatter and the March Hare, before she realized she hadn't had any to drink. "Well, thanks for the tea *party*!"

Alice raced after the White Rabbit. He ran around a corner and when Alice made the turn, he was gone. Finally, Alice decided she wanted to go back home.

She began to run and run. Suddenly, she was floating through space. The next thing she knew, she was under the tree with her cat, Dinah, curled up in her lap. Her sister was still reading to her.

Later that day, Alice was telling Dinah about her adventures in Wonderland. "And can you believe after all that, I didn't get to drink any tea," said Alice. "It's certainly not how *I* would treat a guest."

Then Alice got a wonderful idea. She decided to

 have an unbirthday tea party of her own where she would make sure her guests got to drink all the tea they wanted.

Alice got right down to the planning. "Now, whom should I invite to my party?" she said. She decided not to invite the crazy Mad Hatter or the March Hare because no one would get to drink any tea.

"I will only invite boys and girls who have good manners!" Alice declared.

Dinah looked at Alice and flicked her tail.

"Don't worry, dear Dinah," said Alice. "You're invited to my party, too!"

Happy with her guest list, Alice began to think about the type of invitations she wanted to send. She decided she would draw dainty little teapots and cups and cut them out of colorful paper. Then she would paste them onto the invitations.

On the inside, Alice would write a little poem. "Oh, my! Let's see," said Alice. After a few moments, she came up with this:

As you can see,
It's time for tea.
Please mark the date,
And don't be late!

"I can't let my guests go hungry," said Alice. "What shall I make?"

After some thought, Alice decided to make tea sandwiches with the crusts cut off, cinnamon toast with lots of sugar and raisins, a fruit salad served in pretty bowls, and, of course, lots of berry tea with fresh orange slices.

"Everyone can have as many cups of tea as they like," said Alice.

Alice wasn't sure what she would do with her guests, once their tummies were nice and full, but then she had a wonderful idea.

"A party without games wouldn't be much fun at all," said Alice. First, they'd play hide-and-seek, then ring-around-the-rosy, and finally Alice's favorite game—musical chairs.

Alice just knew it would be so much fun.

When all the delicious food was eaten and all the
games played, it would be time for her guests to leave.

Alice imagined
herself saying
good-bye to
her friends.
She would
curtsy and

thank them dearly for coming to her tea party. And, of
course, her friends would thank her for having such a
fantastic party.

Suddenly, Alice gave a great big yawn. All this planning was certainly making her feel very sleepy. She closed her eyes and in no time she was fast asleep, happily dreaming about the wonderful tea party she was going to have.

Walt Disney's

Snow White
and the Seven Dwarfs

TWO HEARTS AS ONE

Snow White leaned down to kiss her husband, the Prince. "I'll be back soon, dear," she said.

"I will miss you," said the Prince.

Snow White sang happily as she headed toward the Seven Dwarfs' cottage. So much had happened since that long-ago day when the forest animals had led her there. The evil Queen was gone, and Snow White lived happily with her prince. Soon they would celebrate their first wedding anniversary! Snow White could hardly believe it.

"Hello! Hello!" Snow White called out to the Seven Dwarfs as they ran to greet her. Even Grumpy couldn't hide his delight.

"I have a special favor to ask you," said Snow White. "The Prince and I will soon celebrate our first year together. I would like to make him

dinner, but no one at the palace will let me cook!"

"They don't know what they're missin'!" Grumpy exclaimed.

Snow White smiled. "So I wondered if I could make dinner for him here tomorrow night. And I want to give him a special gift—something he could add to his family shield."

"Like a diamond?" asked Doc. "Don't you worry, Snow White. I'll cake tare of it myself. I mean, *take care* of it myself!"

"Oh, thank you so much," she said. "We'll meet here tomorrow evening!"

After Snow White left, Grumpy turned to Doc, and said, "So you don't think the rest of us can find a diamond good enough for Snow White? Well, we'll see about that!"

Grumpy stomped off. All night he planned which part of the mine he would search to find the perfect diamond. He planned for so long that the next morning, he overslept! The others were gone when he woke up. He

rushed out the door—and ran right into the Prince!

"Well, hello, Grumpy," the Prince said, bowing. "I'm glad to find you at home. I have a favor to ask you."

The Prince continued. "Grumpy, I love Snow White so much that I want to give her the most precious gift I

can to celebrate our anniversary. I am having a crown made for her, and I would like to find the most beautiful, most perfect diamond to set in the center of it."

Grumpy couldn't

believe his ears. The Prince was asking him to find a gift for Snow White! Why, if that didn't beat finding a gift for Snow White to give to the Prince, he'd eat his hat! Grumpy puffed up his chest proudly. "I'll find the most beautiful, most sparklin', most dazzlin' diamond in the whole mine!" he cried.

They agreed to meet later that evening.

Meanwhile, deep in the mine, Doc had found his

perfect diamond. Even in the dim light of the mine, the

diamond twinkled like a star. Doc hurried off to tell the

other Dwarfs and to find a pickax to remove the gem.

But Grumpy had also rushed deep into the mine. He turned a corner and stopped. There was the most

beautiful, the most sparkling, the most dazzling diamond in the whole mine. It was the exact same diamond that Doc had found, but Grumpy didn't know that. He didn't want to smudge it, so he hurried off to find a sack for it.

Dopey whistled a little tune to himself. He had been

wandering through the
mine alone, looking for
the perfect diamond
for Snow White. And
there it was! And it
was the very same
diamond that Doc
and Grumpy had
chosen! Carefully,

Dopey dislodged the diamond with his pickax.

Doc, Grumpy, and the other Dwarfs hurried back to

the perfect diamond.

When they got there,

they saw Dopey with

his pickax and the

diamond.

"Dopey!" they

shouted.

Dopey looked up. His pickax slipped and hit the

diamond. Faster than you could say "perfect and

precious," the diamond had broken into two pieces!

"No!" cried Doc and Grumpy. They rushed over and each picked up a piece.

"I was goin' to give it to the Prince for Snow White," said Grumpy.

"Well, I was going to give it to Snow White for the Prince," said Doc.

Far above them at the mine's entrance, the end-of-the-day whistle blew.

"It can't be that late already!" cried Doc. "What will we do? Snow White will be waiting for us when we get home!"

"So will the Prince," said Grumpy.

Doc sighed. "We'll just have to explain."

Grumpy and Doc each put their half into a bag. On the way home, Dopey found some vines to tie the bags shut.

At the Seven Dwarfs' cottage, Snow White had just set the table for their anniversary dinner. The Prince handed her a beautiful bouquet of flowers and kissed her on the cheek.

Snow White wanted to tell him that this dinner was only part of her present, but she just smiled and waited for the Dwarfs to return.

The Prince ate his home-cooked meal slowly, enjoying every bite. Still, as he ate, the Prince wondered what was keeping the Seven Dwarfs. Perhaps they didn't want to disturb Snow White's special dinner. The Prince looked down the path that led to the diamond mine one more time. He couldn't wait to give Snow White her diamond.

Snow White and the Prince were just finishing their pie when the Dwarfs returned. Snow White smiled at Doc. The Prince smiled at Grumpy. Doc carefully set

his bag in front of Snow White, while Grumpy gave his to the Prince.

Snow White and the Prince looked at each

other in surprise.

"This is the other part of my present," said Snow White.

She touched the bag.

The Prince handed Snow White the other bag. "We must think alike," he said. "This is my present for you. It's for your crown. I hope you like it."

Snow White opened the bag. The Prince's eyes widened when he saw the broken diamond.

Grumpy crumpled his cap and frowned.

"Oh, darling, how unusual," said Snow White as she held up the diamond half.

"Yes," said the Prince, disappointed. "Unusual."

"And I have something for you." Snow White beamed as she handed the Prince *her* bag.

The Prince carefully let the diamond drop into his hand.

"Oh, my!" cried Snow White. She looked quickly at Doc, then down at her plate.

The Prince squeezed Snow White's hand. "It's beautiful, my dear, because it is from you," he said.

Then Dopey began playing

a sweet tune on his flute. He

came over to the table and

pointed to Snow White's

diamond and the Prince's

diamond.

"Yes, they are beautiful,

Dopey," said Snow White.

She patted his arm.

Dopey shook his head and

pointed to each of the pieces

again. He looked at the Prince.

"I'm sorry," said the Prince.

"I don't understand."

Dopey set down his flute.

He reached for the Prince's

diamond. Then, he picked

up Snow White's diamond.

And as the Prince and Snow

White watched, he joined the

two separate pieces into one

perfect heart.

The next evening at the anniversary ball, Snow White did not wear her new crown. The Prince did not display his family shield. Instead, they placed the two

pieces of diamond side by side. Snow White and the Prince danced the night away as the beautiful diamond sparkled and shone.

AIM TO PLEASE

"We're back!" cried Cinderella. Through the carriage window, she saw the beautiful white castle glowing in the sunset.

"Welcome home," said the Prince.

Cinderella and the Prince had just been married, and they were returning from their honeymoon.

"I still can't believe I'm going to live in a castle," Cinderella said. "Are you *sure* this isn't just a dream?"

The Prince chuckled. "You're a princess now!" he told his bride. "Princess Cinderella."

They stepped out of the carriage and headed toward the castle. But before they reached the entrance, the King came rushing out.

"Off we go!" he told the Prince. "We have important matters to attend to."

"*Now?*" the Prince said. "Father, I can't just abandon my princess. Not with the royal banquet only two days away. She hasn't had time to prepare!"

"Your Majesty," offered Prudence, the head servant, "I can take care of the preparations, as always—"

"Just show Cinderella what to do," interrupted the King. "We have a princess now. It's *her* duty to plan the banquet." He hurried into the carriage.

"I'm sorry to rush off," said the Prince.

"Don't worry," Cinderella replied. "I'll be fine."

But the next morning, Cinderella wasn't so sure. When she looked in the mirror, she hardly recognized herself with her fancy hairdo and stiff new gown.

"Couldn't I just wear one of my own dresses?" Cinderella asked Prudence and the other servants.

"It simply isn't done," Prudence said haughtily.

Then they took Cinderella to the kitchen for training.

There were

so many

rules to

learn—even

what kind of

dessert to serve at the banquet.

"Stewed prunes," said Prudence.

"Prunes?" exclaimed Cinderella. "For *dessert*?"

"The King expects it," Prudence answered. "It is a

tradition that is *never* broken."

Cinderella's lessons lasted all morning. Every time she tried to suggest one of her own ideas for the banquet, Prudence shook her head and said the same thing—"*It simply isn't done.*" Then she gave Cinderella more rules to follow.

That afternoon, the servants tried to help Cinderella.
They quizzed her about the rules.

"Gold or silver?" they asked. "Fish or fowl? Stand
or sit? Left or right?"

"I—I don't
know!" cried poor
Cinderella.

She was just
about worn out when

she spotted the baker, the flower seller, and some of the
other villagers at the castle gates.

"My friends!" she cried happily. "Open the gates!"

"No, no!" Prudence scolded. "You must remember

the rules.
Commoners
are never
allowed in
the palace.
It simply
isn't done!"
Stunned

by Prudence's remarks, Cinderella ran up to her room.

Once in her room, she started to cry. Cinderella was comforted by her mouse friends. She explained that she was having a hard time understanding all the new rules.

"Especially that rule about keeping commoners out of the palace," she said. "Why, *I* was a dish maid when the Prince married me!"

Suddenly, Cinderella realized that she didn't have to obey anyone's rules about how to act. She was her own person and she could make her own decisions.

"I'm going to plan this banquet *my* way!" Cinderella cried to the mice.

The first step was to let her hair down and put on

her own comfortable clothes. Now Cinderella felt like herself again!

"I know I can do this," she said. "I just have to stop trying to be someone else."

Next, Cinderella marched outside. "Open the gates!"
she cried out.

She walked through the village, passing out banquet

invitations to all

the commoners:

the butcher, the

baker, the flower

seller—dear

friends she had

known her

whole life.

Back at the castle, Cinderella headed straight for the kitchen.

"This party needs help," she said. "Starting with dessert!"

What should she serve? There must be something better than stewed prunes! Then she had a great idea.

"Chocolate pudding!" declared Cinderella. "Now *that* sounds good!"

Cinderella's
next stop was
the ballroom.
There was no
way she was
going to dance
some boring

old dance, even if it *was* the King's favorite. Instead, she

showed the servants a lively waltz.

"We never get to dance like this!" one of the maids

said with a giggle.

Suddenly, Prudence stormed into the ballroom. "It simply isn't done!" she said with a gasp. "IT SIMPLY ISN'T DONE!"

Cinderella tried to reassure her. "I know this is a big change," she said. "But I have to try things my way."

"Well, then," said Prudence, "I certainly hope you know what you're doing."

I hope so, too, thought Cinderella.

It was almost time for the banquet. Cinderella put on *her* favorite dress and *her* favorite necklace. And she fixed her hair just the way *she* liked it. Shortly, she heard carriages rumbling up to the castle.

"It's too late to turn back now," she said.

Cinderella tiptoed downstairs to the ballroom. She was scared to look. What if everyone was having a terrible time?

But it was a wonderful party! The orchestra was playing a merry tune. And the royal guests and commoners were dancing together like the best of

friends. Cinderella quickly joined in and began dancing with the others.

All at once, trumpets began to blow. The King's carriage had arrived!

Cinderella had butterflies in her stomach. What would the King say? Would he be angry about all the changes she had made?

She held her breath as the King walked in. He stopped and stared. Commoners in the palace? The orchestra playing a waltz?

At that moment, a servant ran by with a big silver bowl. *Smack!* He bumped right into the King. *Splat!* The bowl landed right on the King's head!

"What the blazes is going on here?" the King bellowed from beneath the bowl.

"This is all Cinderella's doing!" cried Prudence, standing nearby. "I tried to teach her, but she refused to listen!"

The King pointed to his head. "And what is *this*?"

"Your dessert, sire," whispered Cinderella.

"No prunes?" he cried angrily. Then he took a taste. "Mmmm! Chocolate. My favorite!"

All the servants and guests were staring at the King nervously. Even the orchestra had stopped playing.

Suddenly, the King began to laugh! "What happened to the music?" he called out. "Everybody dance!"

Then he turned to Prudence and Cinderella, who both looked worried. "I always said we needed some new traditions around here. Splendid job. Splendid!"

"It is the princess who deserves your praise, sire," Prudence told him honestly. "And I am honored to be at Her Highness's service."

Cinderella smiled at Prudence. "I think we're going to be great friends."

Just then, the Prince arrived. He swept Cinderella into his arms and gave her a big hug. Then he looked around at all the changes.

"Did I miss something?" he asked.

"Surprise!" cried Cinderella. She then explained everything to him.

The King escorted Cinderella and the Prince over to their thrones.

"I told my son he had chosen well," he announced, beaming at Cinderella. "You're a natural!"

The King slipped a glittery crown onto Cinderella's head.

"Hooray!" everyone cheered.

"Another dance!" ordered the King.

"I'm glad you did things your own way," the Prince told Cinderella.

She blushed. "Someday I'll get this princess thing right."

The Prince leaned over and gave Princess Cinderella a kiss.

"I think that day is today," he answered with a smile.

ARIEL AND THE SEA-HORSE RACE

King Triton, ruler of all the oceans, stormed through the palace courtyard. "Ariel!" he thundered.

Ariel appeared, riding her sea horse, Stormy.

"Daddy, I know what you are going to say—" Ariel began, but King Triton interrupted his daughter, waving a scroll angrily.

"Ariel, how could you sign up for the Annual Sea-Horse Race?" he asked. "No mermaid has ever competed in this race."

"Mermaids ride sea horses, too," she said defiantly. "Stormy may be small, but he's fast. I know we can win if you'll only give us a chance."

"You take too many chances!" King Triton shouted. "I forbid you to enter the race!"

Ariel knew there was no point in arguing. She and Stormy slowly

made their way out of the courtyard.

Ariel's best friend, Flounder, tried to cheer her up.

"That sea-horse trophy isn't so great," he said.

"It just isn't fair!" Ariel cried. "I know I could win!"

"Yes," agreed Flounder. "If you were a merman, your father would let you sign up."

"That's it!" cried Ariel. "I'll be a merman—Arrol, the merman!"

As Ariel went looking for a racing uniform, she swam smack into Sebastian the crab.

"Sorry," said Ariel. "I just have racing on my mind."

"You and your father both," Sebastian said. "He keeps going to the closet to look at his old uniform. He was just your age when he entered his first race."

Ariel stared at Sebastian in shock. Her father used to *race*? She never knew that! And now she knew where to find a uniform!

On the morning of the race, a disguised Ariel nervously joined the other contestants at the starting line.

Finally, King Triton raised his trident, and a spark shot out of it. The riders raced through the water at breakneck speed. When they reached the coral reef, many of the

more powerful sea horses could not fit through the
small openings and had to swim around the reef.

But Stormy was small and Ariel was brave. They
zipped in and out of the spiky coral. It was not long
before they had taken the lead.

As Stormy whipped around the next turn, Ariel's helmet popped off, revealing her long red hair.

A racer named Carpa was right behind her. "A mermaid!" he roared as he roughly pushed Ariel and Stormy.

Stormy was frightened, but he hurried toward the last part of the racecourse: the seaweed hurdles.

Ariel and Stormy swam over and under the hurdles. All of Atlantica could see them now. The crowd gasped as they recognized Ariel. King Triton was shocked.

"You haven't won yet, mermaid!" shouted Carpa.

With one last burst of speed, Stormy raced across the finish line in front of Carpa.

Ariel smiled and waved as the crowd cheered. Then she caught sight of her father looking at her sternly.

Ariel steered Stormy toward her father.

"I'm sorry, Ariel," he said. "I had forgotten how much fun racing could be. Will you forgive me?"

Ariel nodded and kissed his cheek. Then, proudly, King Triton handed the trophy to his daughter—the first mermaid ever to win the Annual Sea-Horse Race.

Disney's
Beauty and the Beast

The Teapot's Tale

Hello! My name is Mrs. Potts. I wasn't always a teapot—heavens, no! Some years ago, a powerful enchantress put everyone who lived in the castle under a strange spell because the Prince was selfish and cruel. All the servants were changed into enchanted objects, and the young Prince was turned into a terrible beast.

The Prince was the only one who could break the spell. The Enchantress gave him a magic rose that would bloom until his twenty-first birthday. The Prince would remain a beast until he could learn to love someone and earn that person's love in return before the rose's last petal fell.

BEAUTY AND THE BEAST

Many lonely years passed while the Beast hid from the world. He refused to leave the castle. He didn't even want any tea! I tried to stay cheerful, but there's nothing sadder than an empty teapot—except an empty teacup like my poor son, Chip.

Then, one stormy day an old man who was lost in the woods found his way to the castle. Lumiere, the candelabrum, and Cogsworth, the mantel clock, let him in and brought him to the fireplace. He was cold and wet, and I was happy to offer him a hot cup of tea.

"It'll warm you up in no time," I said.

But when the Beast came into the room and saw the uninvited guest, he was boiling mad! He hated anyone to see him in his beastly form. "So! You came to stare at the Beast, did you?" he raged.

"I just need a place to stay," the old man explained.

"I'll give you a place to stay!" the Beast roared, and he locked the poor man away in the castle's dungeon.

Beneath his bad temper, I knew the Beast had a kind heart. But I worried that he would never learn to control his temper. And if he didn't learn to love before long, I would stay a teapot forever!

Soon after the old man's arrival, Chip said, "Mama, Mama, there's a girl in the castle!"

"Now, Chip," I scolded, "I'll not have you making up such wild stories."

"Really, Mama! I saw her!" Chip cried.

"Not another word," I said. "Into the tub."

But it was true! The girl's name was Belle, and she had come to rescue her father—the man the Beast had locked away in the dungeon.

Belle was frightened by the Beast, but she offered to stay in her father's place. Her father was very worried, but the Beast didn't seem to care. He sent him home.

Everyone was happy that Belle was staying. She was such a pretty girl. If only she and the master would fall in love and break the spell!

Chip and I went to meet Belle. She seemed so surprised to see us. And it chilled me to the spout to see her so sad. We tried to cheer her up and I, of course,

offered her some tea.

"Now hold still," I said to Chip.

"Thank you," Belle said as she took a sip.

"Changing places with your father was a very brave thing to do," I said. "Things will turn out right in the end. You'll see."

When it was time for dinner, Belle refused to join the Beast. The Beast raged with anger.

"Try to be patient, sir," I said. "After all, the girl has lost her freedom *and* her father in one day."

But the Beast roared, "If she won't eat with me, then she won't eat at all!"

Despite the master's orders, we prepared a wonderful feast for Belle. I'd rather have broken my handle than let such a lovely child go hungry.

The rest of the enchanted objects felt the same way. When Belle came downstairs later that night, we served her the most wonderful meal she had ever eaten.

And Lumiere and the others put on quite a show! They told funny stories and made Belle laugh. We were all trying our best to make her feel at home.

One day, the Beast found Belle in the West Wing. It was the only place in the castle he had forbidden her to visit. The Beast was outraged. He knocked over a table and roared angrily.

Belle was so terrified that she ran away.

But she didn't get far before she was surrounded by a pack of wild wolves. The Beast rescued her, though not before the wolves had clawed and bitten him.

Back at the castle, we watched as Belle tended to the master's wounds. She was very gentle. When she thanked him for saving her life, my eyes steamed with tears and a tingle of hope tickled my spout.

"Perhaps a little love is brewing," I said to Cogsworth and Lumiere.

They nodded their heads in agreement.

And indeed there was! I nearly flipped my lid. For the first time in his life, the master wanted to do something special for someone else. Belle loved to read, so the master told her she could have any of the

books in his

wonderful

library.

Chip was

too young to

understand,

but I knew the

feelings between Belle

and the Beast had changed. I felt all warm inside—even

though I wasn't anywhere near the stove.

Oh, but the course of true love never does run smooth. Belle discovered that her father was ill. She begged the Beast to let her go home, and sadly the master allowed her to leave the castle.

While Belle was taking care of her sick father, trouble began brewing in the village.

Gaston, a
wicked hunter
who also happened
to be in love
with Belle, had
convinced the
villagers that the
Beast would soon

attack their homes. So, they decided to attack the Beast
first. The next thing we knew, the townspeople were
storming the castle.

All the enchanted
objects worked hard
to defend the castle.
But the Beast
wouldn't lift a paw
to help us. He was
heartbroken that
Belle had gone away.

While we tried to get rid of the angry villagers,
Gaston attacked the master. They fought fiercely on the
rooftop of the castle. At first, the Beast couldn't find

the strength to fight back. But then he heard Belle's voice. She had returned.

Finally, the Beast had something to live for. He gathered his strength and grabbed Gaston by the throat.

"Let me go!" cried Gaston.

The Beast

felt sorry for Gaston

and released him.

But as the Beast

turned to embrace

Belle, Gaston

stabbed him in the

back. The Beast

roared in pain. Gaston then tripped and fell off the roof,

never to be seen again. The Beast collapsed.

"Don't leave me. I love you!" cried Belle.

But it was too late. Or was it?

Suddenly, magic sparks filled the air. The Beast

floated off the ground. Rays of light shot from his paws

as they changed into hands and feet. Right in front of

my eyes, the master became a handsome prince once

more!

And I turned into

my old self again, and

so did dear little Chip

and everyone else in

the castle. The curse

over us was broken by the power of true love.

Soon after, we all celebrated with a wonderful ball. The Beast and Belle looked so happy dancing together. "Mama, are Belle and the Prince going to live happily ever after?" Chip asked me.

I nodded and gave him a big hug. "We're going to live happily ever after, too," I said. And I knew we would!

Disney's Aladdin

One True Love

"I'm *baaack*!" yelled the Genie. "Notify the newspapers! The Genie has entered the building!"

"Genie!" Jasmine and Aladdin cried, greeting him with open arms.

Even Rajah gave a little roar.

"How's my favorite couple?" asked the Genie as he put down his suitcase.

"We've missed you," said Aladdin. "How was your trip around the world?"

"It was fabulous!" cried the Genie. "I saw the pyramids in Egypt, went skiing in Sweden, and worked on my tan in the Caribbean—a nice shade of blue, don't you think? I hit every country. Imagine the frequent-flier miles I've built up!

Boy, have I got souvenirs for you both!" the Genie continued. A spark flew from his finger, and soon Aladdin and Jasmine were surrounded by gifts from every country the Genie had visited!

And the Genie had a special surprise for Aladdin, all the way from Australia.

"A kangaroo?" Aladdin gasped. "Oh, Genie, you shouldn't have."

"It was my pleasure," said the Genie.

"No, I mean it—you really shouldn't have!" cried

Aladdin as the kangaroo leaped over the palace wall.

"I'd better go catch it!"

"Be careful!" yelled the Genie. "Kangaroos know

how to box!"

"It's good to have you back," said Jasmine. Then she noticed the Genie looked sad. "What's the matter?" she asked.

"My trip was great, but it got lonely," he said. "I wish I could find a genie to share my life with."

Jasmine put her hand on his shoulder. "I know how that can feel," she said. "I went through a lot of suitors before I found my one true love."

Jasmine began to tell the Genie her story. "I told my father that I wanted to marry for love," she explained. "But the law stated that I had to marry a prince. No matter what I said, my father wouldn't listen. He summoned every suitor he could find to come to court me."

"Sounds like you were pretty popular," the Genie said.

"Popular? Yes," said Jasmine. "Happy? No!

At first, I tried to make the best of the situation," she continued. "I knew my father was counting on me. He ordered tons of beautiful new clothes for me. It was fun in the beginning, trying on one gorgeous outfit after another. The fabrics were incredible: stunning silks and luxurious linens—"

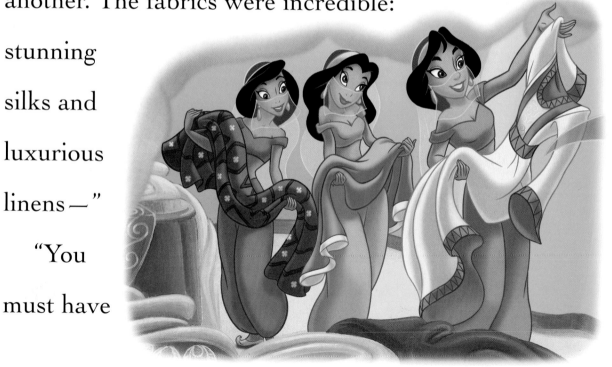

"You must have

looked gorgeous, darling!" interrupted the Genie. "Just like a princess!"

"Genie . . ." Jasmine said in a warning tone.

"Okay, okay, I'll zip it," he said.

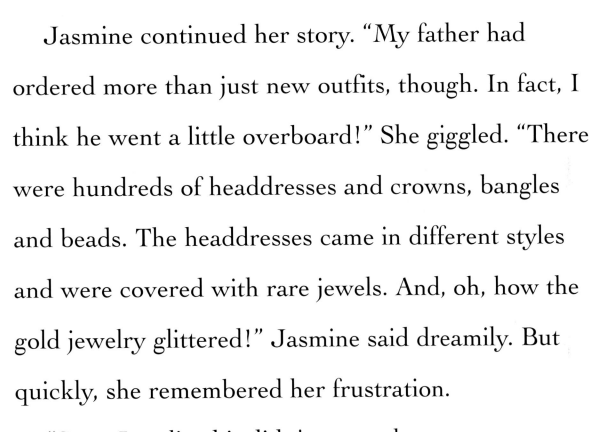

Jasmine continued her story. "My father had ordered more than just new outfits, though. In fact, I think he went a little overboard!" She giggled. "There were hundreds of headdresses and crowns, bangles and beads. The headdresses came in different styles and were covered with rare jewels. And, oh, how the gold jewelry glittered!" Jasmine said dreamily. But quickly, she remembered her frustration.

"Soon I realized it didn't matter how many new outfits I had. What mattered was that I wasn't in love with any of the suitors!"

Then Jasmine told the Genie about her suitors. First there was Prince Achoo (or at least that was the name Jasmine remembered).

"Princess Jasmine," said the prince. "*A-a-a-choo!* It's so—*achoo!*—nice to meet you."

"Oh, dear," said Jasmine. "Are you all right?"

"Yes, yes," said the prince. "Please accept these flowers. *Achoo!*"

"Thank you," Jasmine replied. "They smell beautiful."

"Uh-huh—*achoo!*" agreed the prince. "Um, Princess, are you wearing perfume? *Achoo!*"

"Why, yes, I am," said Jasmine as her eyes grew wide. "Are you allergic to me?"

"*Achoo!* Oh, no, Princess Jasmine!" said the prince. "It's not just you— it seems that I'm allergic to everything in your palace! I must go!"

As the days passed, each suitor seemed worse than the one before, especially Prince Macho.

"I believe a wife should wait on her husband, and be seen and not heard," he said.

"Really?" Jasmine replied. "Well, I prefer a husband who isn't living in the Stone Age!"

Next was Prince Wishy-Washy.

"What do you like to do?" asked Jasmine.

"Whatever *you* like to do," he replied.

"What do you like to eat?" Jasmine asked.

"Whatever *you* like to eat, Princess," he said.

Jasmine decided to have some fun. "We're having roasted ant pitas with rat hummus for lunch."

"Eh . . . delicious," he said hesitantly. "Oh, you know, I just thought of something I have to do. Bye!"

Just when Jasmine had lost hope of finding true love, she met Aladdin. He had helped her escape an angry street vendor after she stole an apple to give to a hungry child. When she met him a second time, he

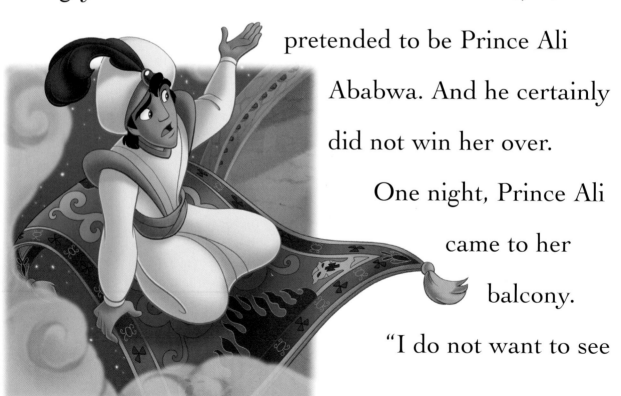

pretended to be Prince Ali Ababwa. And he certainly did not win her over.

One night, Prince Ali came to her balcony.

"I do not want to see

you," Jasmine said. She was tired of feeling like a prize to be won.

"You're right," said Prince Ali. "You aren't just some prize. You should be free to make your own choice."

Soon after, Jasmine discovered that Prince Ali was Aladdin in disguise. And no laws could keep true love from blossoming between them.

Jasmine noticed that the Genie was bawling.

"That was the sweetest story I've ever heard!" he

cried.

Jasmine laughed.

"You can find the same

happiness that Aladdin

and I share. I just know

your special genie is out

there!" she said.

"But what if she isn't?" asked the Genie.

"But what if she *is*?" said Jasmine.

Just then, Aladdin showed up with the kangaroo. "That kangaroo sure has a strong right punch," he said, holding his sore arm.

"No time to talk, Al," said the Genie, rushing out the door. "I've got a genie to find—and not a thing to wear!"

"What's with him?" Aladdin asked Jasmine.

"He wants to have what we have," said Jasmine. She smiled at Aladdin. "True love."

Within minutes, the Genie reappeared. He put on a quick fashion show for Jasmine and Aladdin. "Do I go for the handsome banker look? Or the tuxedo look? Or

maybe the preppy, golf-player look? Or perhaps the surfer look? Which one do you think works best?" he asked.

"You want someone to like you for who you are on the inside," said Jasmine. "Just be yourself."

A lightbulb went off above the Genie's head.

"Presto change-o!" he shouted, and all the clothes vanished. He stood in front of them, wearing his usual outfit. "How do you like my new . . . er . . . old look?"

"It suits you perfectly," Jasmine said with a smile.

"How about a ride on the Magic Carpet?" Aladdin asked Jasmine as soon as the Genie had left.

"I'd love it," replied Jasmine.

As they flew away from Agrabah, Jasmine snuggled close to Aladdin. Suddenly, in the distance, she saw a blanket and food set up on the top of a mountain.

As they landed, Jasmine exclaimed, "Our own private picnic—on our own private mountain!"

"Do you like it?" asked Aladdin.

"Of course!" cried Jasmine. "Oh, Aladdin! I'm so lucky to have you!"

Aladdin shook his head. "No, I'm the lucky one," he said, giving Jasmine a hug.

As they enjoyed their sunset picnic, Jasmine thought again about all those suitors she had met. Because of them, she was able to appreciate the gift of true love that she had finally found with Aladdin.

"It's been quite a day," said Aladdin.

"And there's no one I'd rather spend it with than you," Jasmine said.

Walt Disney's Sleeping Beauty

A Moment to Remember

Princess Aurora sighed. She loved Prince Phillip, but life in the palace was so different. Tonight there would be yet another royal ball, and the fairies, Flora, Fauna, and Merryweather, were bickering over what she should wear.

Aurora looked out the window. She missed the quiet glade where she had met Phillip.

"Merryweather, I told you Aurora didn't want to wear that dress. This one will look much better," said Fauna as she gestured to the gown.

And as soon as Fauna turned her back, Merryweather tried to change the color of the gown.

"Now, dears," said Flora, "let's not argue. We all know this pink dress suits Aurora best. Don't you think so, Aurora?"

Before Aurora could answer, the Royal Chef entered the room to show the princess an ice sculpture. As she smiled her approval, a castle maid hurried in to tell Aurora that they were almost out of candles. As Aurora finished telling her to check the storeroom, Prince Phillip came into the room.

"Hello, dearest," he said, giving Aurora a hug.

"Oh, Phillip, I'm so glad to see you. I . . ." Aurora began.

"A-hem." The Royal Florist cleared his throat. "Princess Aurora, could you please tell the Royal Table Setter that these flowers are to be placed in the middle of each table tonight?"

"Princess," said the Royal Table Setter, "could you please tell the Royal Florist that our guests will never see one another if I put his big flower arrangements in the middle of each table?"

"Why don't you just put a single flower on each

table?" said Aurora.

The two servants looked horrified. "A single flower?" they said as they left.

"You were saying, dear?" Phillip asked.

"Pardon me, Princess Aurora," said the Royal

Steward. "I must have

your approval on the

seating arrangements."

"I will look at them—"

Princess Aurora began.

"As soon as we

return," Prince Phillip finished.

"Where are we going, Phillip?" Aurora asked.

"For a ride where no one can bother us," Phillip said.

After changing into their riding clothes, Aurora and

Phillip went to the royal stable. The Royal Groom led

out Mirette, Aurora's horse, and Samson, Phillip's horse.

"Oh, Phillip, this was such a good idea," said Aurora.

"I'm sorry, dearest. I had forgotten that the Royal

Equestrian Guard must come with us," Phillip said.

Aurora tried to hide her disappointment. Then she

leaned over and whispered to Samson. Whinnying,

Samson charged away from the palace with Phillip.

Mirette dashed after them, leaving the Royal Equestrian

Guard far behind.

A MOMENT TO REMEMBER

"Whooaa! Whoa, Samson!" Phillip shouted as Samson raced ahead.

"It's all right, Phillip!" Aurora called. "Samson knows where he's going."

They galloped into the forest, where Samson found a path through the trees. Then he left the path and stopped suddenly.

SPLASH! Phillip sailed over Samson's head and landed in a stream.

"No carrots for you, boy!" Prince Phillip scolded his horse. He looked around and noticed some familiar-looking forest animals. Then he saw Aurora

sliding out of the saddle. She smiled down at him.

"Do you remember this place, Phillip?" Aurora

asked.

Phillip sloshed out of the stream and sat down on a rock. He took off his cape and pulled off his boots to dump the water out of them.

Aurora took off her shoes and cape. She spun around gracefully, humming a tune.

"Yes," Prince Phillip said softly. "I remember this place. . . ."

"I will never

forget that day," said Aurora, "no matter how busy our lives become."

Prince Phillip smiled and touched her face. "Nor will I.

For when I am with you, everything else disappears."

Phillip and Aurora smiled, wishing they could bring the joy and contentment they had known in the glade back to the palace.

Their peaceful moment ended abruptly as the Royal Equestrians thundered into the glade.

"I'm sorry, Prince Phillip," said the Head Guardsman. "We followed as quickly as we could. I hope you have not come to any harm."

"No harm done," said Phillip as he put on his boots, hat, and cape.

"We can take one more minute, dear," whispered
Phillip. "I can send them back ahead of us."
Apologetically, he picked up a fallen flower and handed
it to Aurora.

Aurora took the
flower and smiled.
"No, Phillip," she said.
"There is so much to
do to prepare for
tonight. We should
go back."

Aurora put on her shoes and cape, and climbed into Mirette's saddle. She had a wonderful idea! If she worked quickly, she could surprise Phillip that night.

Phillip touched Aurora's hand and said, "You go ahead, dear. I'll send half of the guard with you. I will be back soon."

Aurora nodded and smiled. Yes, that would allow her to get a head start on her plan.

Phillip watched as Aurora trotted away. He had an idea of his own. If he worked quickly and carefully, he could surprise Aurora that night.

"Not a word of this to the princess," he said to her animal friends as he gathered some flowers.

Aurora did not see Prince Phillip for the rest of the afternoon. She was too busy working on his surprise. Under her watchful eye, servants carefully arranged

flowers and food, and brought candles to the tables. The fairies flitted about, helping wherever they could.

More than once, Aurora heard a servant murmur, "Our guests will certainly be . . . surprised."

Aurora just smiled. "It is Prince Phillip I want to surprise," she told the servants. "Not a word of this to him."

The servants nodded. Prince Phillip's valet hurried off to keep the prince away.

That night, the fairies helped Aurora dress in a gown she had picked herself.

Then, Prince Phillip came into the room, holding a simple wreath of flowers from the glade. "Would you like to wear this, too?" he asked.

"Oh, Phillip!" Aurora put on the flower crown and hugged her husband. "It is perfect for this evening."

"And now I have a surprise for you!" she cried as she led Phillip down the stairs to the ballroom. It was dark and empty.

"You've canceled the ball?" Prince Phillip asked. "Have the guests left?"

"No, Phillip," Aurora said, touching her flower crown. "You brought our little glade back to me. Now, let me take you back to our little glade."

Aurora led Phillip into the courtyard. A sweet

breeze whispered through the trees. Water danced in

the fountain, sounding like a mountain stream. Candles

flickered in the darkness, and the stars

twinkled in the sky above them.

"The glade will always be in our hearts,"

Aurora whispered. "But now it is in our palace,

too."

Prince Phillip took Princess Aurora's hand.

"Then we should dance," he said.

Just then Phillip's father, King Hubert,

entered the courtyard. "I say," he said with a chuckle. "This is much better than the stuffy balls I usually attend!"

While their animal friends watched, Princess Aurora and Prince Phillip happily danced the night away in their new glade.

Disney's
ATLANTIS
THE LOST EMPIRE

KIDA AND THE CRYSTAL

Far out in the Atlantic Ocean, a huge tidal wave formed. It was headed right for the city of Atlantis!

The people of Atlantis ran for shelter, but it was hopeless. The wave was about to swallow up their

island!

This can't be happening, the king thought. Atlantis was a great and powerful city. How could it be in danger?

The queen saw the fear in the king's eyes. "Come quickly, Kida!" she cried to their  young daughter. But Princess Kida lagged behind. She had dropped her doll.

Suddenly, a red light filled the sky. The light came from a giant Crystal that was floating above the city.

All at once, the light turned into a blue beam and fell upon the queen. The light pulled her into the Crystal.

"Mama!" Kida cried as her hand slipped out of her mother's. But it was too late. The queen had already disappeared into the Crystal.

Then more beams of blue light shot down from the Crystal, surrounding Atlantis like a bubble.

Finally, the tidal wave hit! It crashed against the bubble. The city was safe. Then the island

of Atlantis began to sink, down, down, down, deep into the ocean and away from the rest of the world.

Atlantis was saved, but it was no longer a great city. Now it was a lost empire, hidden beneath the sea!

Many years passed, and Princess Kida grew into a beautiful young woman. She had long white hair and wide blue eyes. And like all Atlanteans, she wore a crystal around her neck.

"She looks just like her father," the people of Atlantis would whisper. They thought Kida wasn't listening, but the princess was *always* listening — and learning.

Kida was eager to know why Atlantis had sunk into the ocean. She also wanted to find out more about an old memory she had—about a bright light that filled the sky. But mostly she wanted to know what had happened to her mother. She decided to go speak with her father.

"Father, tell me about the Great Flood," she begged.

But as always, the king refused to talk about the past, and he would not share the secrets of Atlantis with Kida. "We cannot change our history," he told his daughter.

"Maybe by learning about the past, we can help Atlantis grow strong again," Kida said.

"Enough, Kida!" her father exclaimed.

Angrily, Kida grabbed her spear and ran down the palace steps. She headed for a maze of caves where she often hunted for cave beasts. But instead of finding cave beasts, she discovered something much more interesting—

explorers from the surface world!

"Welcome to Atlantis," Kida said. "Come, you must speak with my father."

When Kida brought the explorers to her father, he was not happy to see them at all. He wanted them to leave Atlantis right away.

"These people may be able to help us," said Kida.

The king shook his head. He insisted that the visitors depart the very next day.

Kida was disappointed with her father's decision, but she had an idea. Outside the throne room, she stopped one of the explorers. His name was Milo.

"I have some questions for you," Kida told him. "And I will not let  you leave this city until they're answered!"

Milo was just as curious about Atlantis as the princess was. He agreed to help her.

Kida then told Milo what she remembered about the
Great Flood.

"You were there?" he cried. "That would make you
more than eight thousand years old!"

"Yes," Kida said.

"Looking good,"
Milo joked.

Next, it was Milo's
turn to share. He showed
Kida an ancient book about
Atlantis called *The Shepherd's Journal.*

Milo said it was his dream to find out what had happened to the city.

"It is my dream, too," said Kida. Then she admitted something to Milo—she couldn't read the book.

"Since the Great Flood, no one has been able to read," she said sadly. "Our history has been lost."

Next, Kida showed Milo around the city.

"Are you hungry?" asked Kida.

"I sure am!" cried Milo. Then he saw what Kida was buying—gooey tentacles on sticks!

"I sure am . . . not hungry anymore," he added quickly.

But Kida made him take a bite.

"Not bad!" he said.

"Could use some ketchup."

Next, Milo and Kida played an Atlantean game.

"You knock down the fish statues with this ball,"

explained Kida.

Crash! Milo hit

all the statues.

"That was

great!" cried Kida.

"Well, I *am* the

champ at Bowl 'n'

Burp Lanes," Milo

said proudly.

"Kida! Kida!" A little girl ran up to Kida and Milo.

"Hello, Tali." Kida gave the girl a big hug.

"You're coming to my birthday party, right?" asked Tali.

"Of course," answered Kida. "A girl doesn't turn fifteen hundred every day."

Milo had a fun time at the party. He especially liked meeting the Atlantean people.

Then it was time for Tali's birthday cake. Kida started to laugh as she watched Milo try to eat. "Um . . . Milo," she told him, "you're using an Atlantean hairbrush to eat your cake."

The cake tasted even better when Milo ate it with an Atlantean fork!

After the party, Milo and Kida hiked to the top of a hill overlooking the city. Milo gazed down at Atlantis.

"The most my team hoped to find was some crumbling buildings," he told Kida. "Instead, we found a whole city full of people!"

But the princess shook her head. She explained that her people were in trouble. The city was slowly falling apart, and it was getting harder to find food. And every year the people of Atlantis forgot more of their history.

Kida then led Milo to a pool of water. "I brought you to this place to ask for your help," she said.

"Follow me," Kida instructed as she dove deep into the water. Milo followed close behind. Soon they swam past the ruins of ancient Atlantean buildings where colorful murals and writings covered the walls.

Milo could hardly believe his eyes. The murals and writings told the whole story of Atlantis!

"This is amazing!" Milo said when they came up for air. "The history of Atlantis is painted on these walls!"

Kida could hardly speak. At last she would learn about her people, and maybe she would even discover what had happened to her mother!

"Does the writing say anything about the light I saw?" Kida asked.

They both took a deep breath and dove back under the water. Milo found the words and drawings that explained all about the Crystal.

When they came back up, Milo told Kida what he had found out.

"The Crystal is the Heart of Atlantis," Milo said. "It is a power source. It keeps everyone and everything in Atlantis alive."

Kida nodded slowly. She was beginning to understand why her father wouldn't talk about the past—why he kept the Heart of Atlantis a secret. He feared that its great power would be misused.

Kida remembered the last time she saw the huge Crystal. Her mother had floated up into its blue light. As soon as she had disappeared, Atlantis had been saved from the tidal wave.

Now Kida understood something else, too. Her mother was a hero. She had given her life for the sake of the city!

Kida hugged Milo. "Thank you for your help," she said. Milo blushed. The princess smiled. Not only had she found out the truth about Atlantis but she had also made a wonderful new friend!

As Milo turned to swim back, Kida took another

long look at the

pictures on the walls.

They showed the

history of her

city—and told the

story of her family.

"Thank you,

Mother," she

whispered, "for all you

have done for us."

Just then, Kida's crystal necklace began to glow.

She knew it was a message from her mother.

"Be brave," the crystal seemed to say. "Be strong."

And Kida was. With Milo's help, she was ready to unlock *all* the secrets of Atlantis. Her adventure was just beginning!

DISNEY'S

CINDERELLA II
Dreams Come True

AN UNCOMMON ROMANCE

*T*hey *lived happily ever after.* . . .

Anastasia gazed at the prince and princess on her music box and sighed. Her own stepsister, Cinderella, had found a prince to marry—and now she lived in a castle! Why couldn't Anastasia be so lucky? Instead,

she was stuck at home with her bossy mother and her crabby sister, Drizella.

"Girls!" shrieked Anastasia's mother. "Cinderella's ball is tomorrow night. Every noble bachelor in the kingdom will be there! If you want to find a husband, you have to make the most

of this opportunity. I won't let you fail me . . . *again.*"

"Yes, Mother," the sisters said obediently.

"Drizella, pin back those curls! Anastasia, put more color in your cheeks!" their mother demanded as they

got ready to go out. "A perfect appearance is the *only* way to attract a proper gentleman."

As the girls followed their mother's orders, they talked about the rich, royal men they hoped to meet at Cinderella's ball.

"Maybe a count!" Anastasia said dreamily.

"Or a duke!" added Drizella.

"Precisely," their mother said. "We shall find you men of wealth *and*

nobility. Come along, now. We need new gowns for the both of you."

Then they headed into the village.

Meanwhile, at the castle, Princess Cinderella was getting ready to go to the village, too. She put on an old dress and tied a scarf in her hair. The princess didn't want anyone to recognize her, because she had a very secret errand to do.

"I want to surprise the Prince with a garland of flowers," she confided to her mice friends along the way. Cinderella had heard about a special tradition—if

a man and woman gave each other a garland at a ball, it meant they would be together forever.

Cinderella wasn't the only one with garlands on her mind. Anastasia couldn't help glancing at the flower seller's wares as she passed by. Before she knew what she was doing, she was standing in front of his cart.

"Remember the tradition!" the flower seller told her. "Don't you need a garland for the ball?"

Anastasia shook her head sadly. After all, she had no one to give it to.

"Anastasia!" her mother bellowed. "What are you doing?"

"Nothing!" cried Anastasia. "I'm coming!"

Anastasia knew she should hurry and catch up with the others. But she couldn't help stopping again outside the bakery. The fresh bread smelled wonderful!

She closed her eyes and followed her nose into the

shop. She didn't notice the Baker pulling a batch of rolls out of the oven.

BUMP! Anastasia knocked right into the Baker. Her eyes

met his. And in an instant, she felt something magical happen!

At that very moment, Cinderella walked by. She couldn't believe what she saw  through the shop window. Could it be that her stepsister was falling in love?

"Everything smells . . . so good!" Anastasia stammered.

"Would you like one?" asked the Baker, holding out a basket of hot rolls.

Anastasia blushed. She nodded shyly and took a roll.

Just then, *WHACK!* Anastasia's mother knocked the

bread out of her hand.

"Anastasia, I think *not*,"

her mother said icily.

"Everything in this shop

is . . ." She stopped and

glanced down her nose

at the Baker. ". . . *inferior*."

Outside on the street, she scolded Anastasia. "You're

not to say another word to that shopkeeper. I forbid it!"

"Yes, Mother," mumbled Anastasia.

A little while later, Cinderella found Anastasia kneeling at the village well, alone and crying.

"I saw you in the Baker's shop," Cinderella said quietly.

Anastasia told Cinderella that she had

fallen in love with the Baker. "But Mother forbids it!" cried Anastasia. "She thinks he's beneath me."

"I think she's wrong," said Cinderella. "The Baker's terrific!"

For a moment, Anastasia cheered up. Then she grew miserable again. She didn't believe the Baker could love her back.

"I'm so clumsy and plain," she sobbed.

"Don't give up!" exclaimed Cinderella. She knew

that dreams could come true—with a little help! "Why don't you come back to the castle with me?"

At the castle, Cinderella dried Anastasia's tears and fixed her hair. She found a pretty dress and necklace for

Anastasia to wear.

"There," said Cinderella.

"Don't stop now," said Anastasia. "Mother says looks count for everything!"

Cinderella frowned. "Well, of course you want to look your best. But that's not the important thing. The way to impress the Baker is just to be nice to him."

"You think so?" asked Anastasia. "But what if Mother catches me? She

told me never to speak to him again!"

"Maybe it's time to stop following someone else's orders," said Cinderella, "and start following your heart."

Anastasia knew Cinderella was right. The next day, she bought a garland from the flower seller.

She was going to ask the Baker to the ball!

Anastasia didn't know it, but the Baker had bought a garland, too. He was planning on asking *her* to the ball!

The Baker showed his garland to one of his customers. "Do you think she'll like it?" he asked.

"She'll love it!" the woman promised.

Just then, Anastasia turned the corner and saw the Baker with the woman. It looked like he was offering her a garland! Anastasia gasped. He's in love with someone else! she thought.

Anastasia threw down her garland and ran away, sobbing.

"Anastasia!" cried the Baker as he saw her running away. He raced all over the market, looking for her. At

last, feeling hopeless, he sat down by the fountain. Even his garland looked sad. Nothing was left but a single, straggly flower.

Then, from the other side of the fountain, he heard a sniffle. It was Anastasia! Her face was streaked with tears.

"Don't look at me," she said. "I look horrible!" She got up to run away again, but the Baker took her hand.

"Wait! Please!" begged the Baker. He offered

Anastasia the only thing he had—the leftover flower.

Anastasia was so surprised, she hardly knew what to

do. Then

she broke

into a wide

smile. She

took the

flower

from the Baker and tucked it in her hair. The two of

them leaned toward each other, and . . .

"*ANASTASIA!*" A shrill voice rang out. It was her mother!

"How dare you defy me?" she yelled, snatching the flower out of Anastasia's hair. "You were forbidden to speak to this man!"

Cinderella was in the market, too, and heard all the commotion. She ran to the fountain just in time to hear her stepmother say, "You deserve better. Come along!"

Cinderella sighed. She couldn't bear to see Anastasia

give in to her mother again. But then she heard some-thing surprising.

"No, Mother!" declared Anastasia. "You're wrong."

Anastasia took the Baker by the hand. "We're going to the ball . . . *together*."

Anastasia's mother was furious and stomped away in a huff.

That night at the ball, Anastasia whirled around the dance floor with the Baker. As Cinderella and the Prince waltzed past them, Anastasia said, "Thank you. I never dreamed I could be this happy!"

"You see," said Cinderella. "Dreams do come true!"

Anastasia and the Baker danced all night. And after that . . .

They lived happily ever after!

DISNEY'S THE LITTLE MERMAID

DREAMS UNDER THE SEA

Ariel's secret grotto was her favorite place in the whole undersea world—especially now that the statue of Prince Eric was there.

"Oh, Flounder, it's almost like having Eric with me!" Ariel cried to her best friend, as she threw her arms around the statue's neck.

"Ariel!" Sebastian the crab exclaimed. "Get a hold of yourself. He's not real. He's nothing but a hunk of rock!"

Ariel put her ear up to the statue's mouth. "Did you say something, Eric?" she asked. She pretended to listen for a moment, then turned to her friends. "He said that if you two would please excuse us for a moment, he has something he'd like to say to me alone. Go on. Shoo!"

Ariel placed her head on the statue's shoulder and pretended to answer his proposal. "Why, yes, I'd love to marry you, Eric," she said.

"Marry?" Sebastian roared. "You will do no such thing. In the name of His Royal Highness,

King Triton, I forbid this kind of talk."

"Sebastian," Ariel said, "it's a statue, remember? I'm just playing make-believe. Please don't tell my father, okay?"

Sebastian reluctantly shook his head. "I just know I'm going to regret this," he moaned.

"We can have the wedding in here tomorrow morning," Ariel said. "Will you both help me?"

"Help you with what?" Sebastian asked. "It's make-believe. You said so yourself."

"Oh, dream weddings are every bit as much work as real weddings," Ariel said, handing Sebastian an armful of seaweed to decorate the grotto. "Everything has to be just right!

"I think Prince Eric is perfectly dressed for a wedding," Ariel continued as she began decorating the grotto.

"The real Prince Eric is *human*," Sebastian said. "He lives on land! And every self-respecting sea dweller knows that mermaids LIVE UNDERWATER!"

"That may be true," Ariel replied. "But who knows what the future will bring?"

"May I be the chef?" Flounder asked. "Please, please?"

Ariel laughed. "Of course, Flounder," she said. "I want you to

prepare all the most wonderful foods you can imagine."

"Seaweed soufflé . . . plankton pie . . ." Flounder said happily.

"Oh, yes!" Ariel cried. "And don't forget the wedding cake!"

"A huge cake!" Flounder exclaimed.

"With a different flavor for each layer," Ariel said.

"Just leave it to me," Flounder said proudly. "This will be a wedding feast like no one has ever seen!"

"You can say that again," Sebastian muttered.

"Oh, I can hardly wait!" Ariel exclaimed. "I can picture the entire ceremony. My sisters will make such beautiful bridesmaids. And my father will look so proud and distinguished as we—"

"Your sisters . . . your father . . ." Sebastian sputtered, looking as if he were ready to faint.

"Oh, don't be such a party pooper, Sebastian," Ariel said lightly. "It's only pretend, after all."

But then Ariel said to herself, "But someday it's going to be real. I just know that someday my dream will come true!"

"I'm leaving," Sebastian said. "I can't take any more of this nonsense!"

"Flounder," Ariel called, "can you think of someone else to be the master conductor of the grand orchestra and perform the ceremony?"

"Master conductor? Perform the ceremony?" Sebastian asked, stopping in his tracks.

"You're my first choice," Ariel said. "But . . ."

"BUT nothing!" Sebastian cried. "A crab must do what a crab must do. The wedding—must go on!"

Grabbing a candlestick, Sebastian began to conduct the imaginary orchestra.

"May I have this dance, Ariel?" Flounder asked, bowing politely.

"With pleasure," Ariel said, laughing. She and Flounder waltzed and twirled until they were both too dizzy to dance anymore.

That evening, in her room, Ariel was trying on her veil, which she had made from a curtain, when there was a knock at her door. It was Flounder and he was holding a long string of pearls.

"Oh, Flounder, they're beautiful!" Ariel gasped with delight.

"They belong to a friend of mine," Flounder said. "She said you could borrow them."

Now Ariel had *something old* (the dinglehopper to comb her hair), *something new* (her veil), *something borrowed* (the pearls), and *something blue* (her blue shell bracelet). "That's everything a bride needs!" she cried happily.

The next morning, Sebastian escorted Ariel to the

grotto, where Flounder
was waiting for them.

"Gee, Ariel," he said.
"You look great!"

"Are you sure you
want to go through with this?" Sebastian asked.

"Not getting cold feet—uh—claws, are you,
Sebastian?" Ariel said teasingly.

"Nothing of the kind!" Sebastian sniffed. "The
orchestra and I will be ready when you are."

A few minutes later, they heard loud sounds coming from inside the grotto. Flounder peeked in and saw Sebastian conducting the orchestra.

"I'm not sure, but I think Sebastian has started playing the wedding march," he said. "Are you ready?"

Ariel nodded, and Flounder escorted her into the grotto.

"Dum-dum-de-dum, dum-dum-de-dum, dum-dum-de-dum-dum-de-dum-dum-de-dum . . ." Sebastian sang as he conducted the orchestra. He stopped abruptly when he caught sight of Ariel.

"Ohhhhhh," wailed Sebastian, sniffing loudly and wiping a tear from his eye as Ariel took her place next to the statue. "Weddings always make me cry!"

Then, clearing his throat importantly, Sebastian

asked, "Do you, Princess Ariel, take this . . . er . . . this

statue to be

your—now

listen closely to

this part, young

lady—MAKE-

BELIEVE

husband?"

"I do!" Ariel

cried happily.

"And do you, Mr. Pretend Prince, take this perpetually provoking princess to be your make-believe wife?" Sebastian finished.

Ariel leaned toward Eric. "He says he does," she said.

"Well, then, I pronounce you one hundred percent IMAGINARY husband and wife," Sebastian said.

"Hooray!" Flounder cheered, as he rushed to catch Ariel's bouquet.

With her eyes glowing like stars, Ariel hugged her friends. "Oh, thank you! This has been a dream wedding!" she cried. "And now I'm inviting you both to

my *real* wedding to Prince Eric. I'm not sure when it will happen—or where or how— but I know it *will* happen. I can feel it in my heart."

Sebastian opened his mouth to speak, and Ariel put her finger to his lips to stop him.

"It won't matter that there's an ocean of difference between us," Ariel said. "Nothing will stand in the way of true love."

"Nothing," Flounder agreed dreamily.

Ariel smiled and closed her eyes, imagining a kiss from Prince Eric. . . .

"Ewwwwwwww!" she cried as she realized that she was actually kissing Flounder.

"Aaahh!" Flounder screamed at the same time.

"Aha!" Sebastian shouted. "See what comes of silly notions about marrying human princes . . . as if that could ever really happen. . . ."

But Ariel knew that someday her dream would come true.

Beautifully illustrated volumes filled with magical Disney stories

0-7868-3402-1

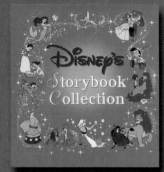

0-7868-3234-7

0-7868-3247-9

0-7868-3359-9

Collections for every family to treasure!

0-7868-3342-4

0-7868-3444-7

$15.99 each!
($19.99 CAN)

Collect Them All!

0-7868-3260-6

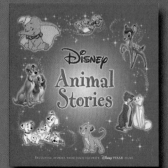

0-7868-3257-6

0-7868-3290-8

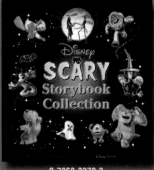

0-7868-3379-3

© Disney

 Disney PRESS   Visit us at www.disneybooks.com • Available at bookstores and retailers everywhere